14 OF THE MOST TERRIBLE
CHILDREN'S BOOKS EVER WRITTEN

Copyright © 2020 Brad Gosse
Images courtesy
Vectortoons.com

All rights reserved.

ISBN: 9798550554609

AFTER GOING PEE

YOUR MOTHER MADE IT VERY CLEAR

GERMS ARE WHAT WE HAVE TO FEAR

POOP CONTAINS THE ECOLI

A BACTERIA THAT MIGHT MAKE YOU DIE

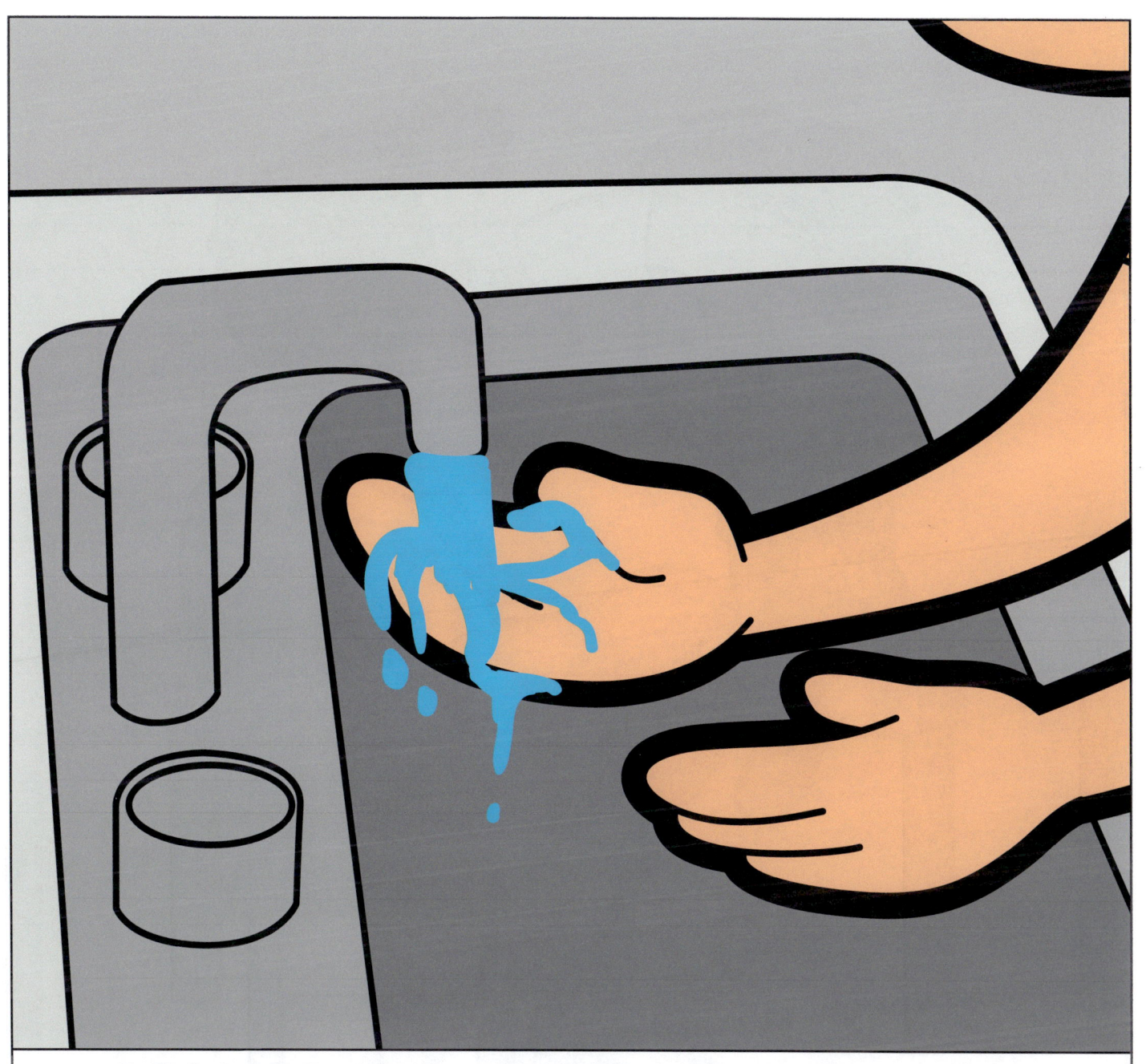

BECAUSE YOUR HANDS. YOU WOULD NOT CLEAN

IT'S ALL YOUR FAULT

THAT YOU GOT SICK

YOU NEVER LISTEN. YOU LITTLE PRICK

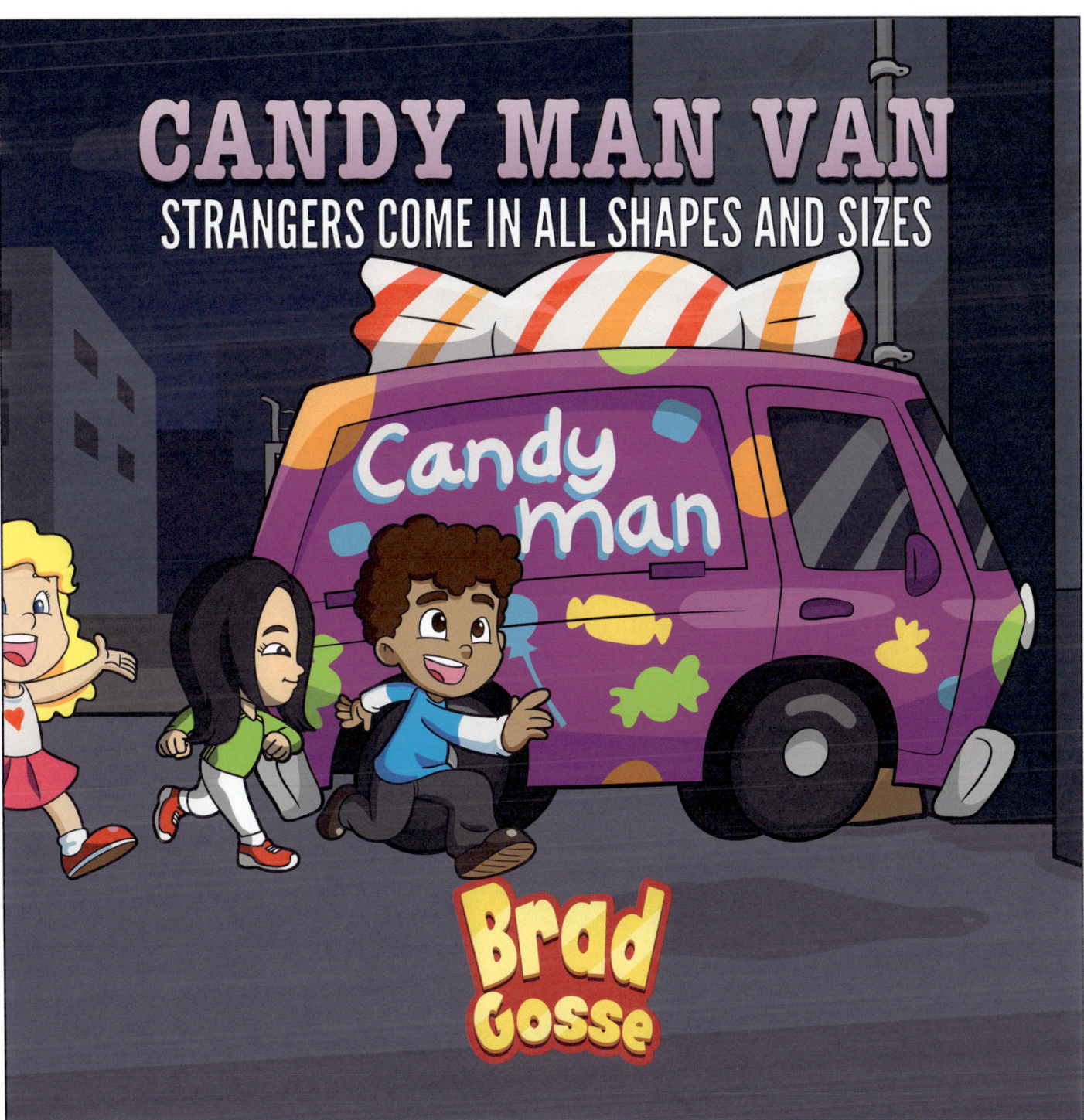

WHEN WE THINK OF STRANGERS WE PICTURE A VAN

SOMETIMES WE PICTURE A DIRTY OLD MAN

SOMETIMES YOUR MOM'S SICK

BUT THEY DON'T LOOK AT ALL LIKE SEX OFFENDER RANDY

CINNAMON IS A SPECIAL HORSE

HE'S ALWAYS HAPPY TO RUN. OF COURSE

CINNAMON WINS ALL THE RACES

HE PUTS SMILES ON PEOPLE'S FACES

CINNAMON HAS A GOOD CAREER

RETIREMENT WILL SOON BE NEAR

UNTIL CINNAMON BROKE HIS LEG

AND NOW HE WILL BE FORCED TO PEG

LADY HORSES ALL DAY LONG

CINNAMON WILL BE USED FOR HIS DONG

AS HE GETS READY FOR HIS DAILY JERK

HE REALIZES. THAT THIS IS SEX WORK.

ONCE HE WAS THE STAR OF THE SHOW

CINNAMON HAS BECOME A HO

DADDY'S A SIMP
DON'T EXPECT MUCH INHERITANCE

Brad Gosse

WHEN YOUR MOMMY DIED

YOUR DAD HAD IT ROUGH

HE GOT HIMSELF RIGHT. EVEN THOUGH IT WAS TOUGH.

SO HE SET HIMSELF UP WITH A DATING PROFILE

HE SHAVED OFF HIS STUBBLE

AND POLISHED HIS SMILE

IT'S BEEN A LONG TIME SINCE YOUR DAD WENT ON DATES

AND HE CAME HOME HAPPY.
EVERYTHING TURNED OUT GREAT

BUT THINGS SEEM STRANGE WITH YOUR DADS NEW LADY

HE'S TAKING HER ON LOTS OF BIG SHOPPING TRIPS LATELY

SHE'S NOT EVEN AFFECTIONATE WITH YOUR DEAR OLD DAD

ALWAYS TOO TIRED FOR SEX AND THAT'S BAD

AND THEN SOMETHING HAPPENED THAT SEEMS KINDA STRANGE

HE BOUGHT HER A HOUSE. JUST A FEW BLOCKS AWAY

HIS GIRLFRIEND WON'T TOUCH HIM. SHE CALLS HIM A WIMP

I'M SORRY TO TELL YOU YOUR DADDY'S A SIMP

DEAD BABIES 2

A SERIES OF SHORT LIFE STORIES

Brad Gosse

MEERA WAS TRAPPED UNDERNEATH THE ICE

SAM HAD A FATAL ACCIDENT FALLING OFF HIS BIKE

KURT WAS CHEWED UP AND
EATEN BY HIS DOG

DIGGING THROUGH THE TRASH IS HOW WE LOST DOUG

MARK SLIPPED AND FELL ON A FRESH WET FLOOR

DEATH BY ELECTROCUTION KILLED BABY THOR

AVA DIED CHOKING ON HER
FAVORITE TOY

A BOTCHED SURGERY CAUSED THE DEATH OF THIS BOY

MANDEEP WAS KILLED IN A BIG HOUSE FIRE

THIS GIRL WAS CRUSHED
UNDERNEATH A CAR TIRE

THEO DRANK TOO MUCH
HOUSEHOLD POISON

CONSTIPATION AND SEPSIS IS HOW WE LOST ROYSTON

MARY DIED INSIDE THE WASHING MACHINE

A LEG HOLD TRAP ENDED THE LIFE OF BABY EUGENE

ALICE WAS FOUND IN A PUDDLE FACE DOWN

CHUCK CRASHED HIS CAR ON HIS WAY DOWNTOWN

ELAINE FELL DOWN AND CRACKED OPEN HER HEAD

NOBODY KNOWS HOW DAVE WOUND UP DEAD

HELEN HAD A TRAGIC FALL
DOWN THE BACK STAIRS

*SUFFOCATION BY PLASTIC BAG
IS HOW WE LOST BABY BLAIR*

Make Your Own Luck

PRACTICAL MONEY ADVICE FOR KIDS

Brad Gosse

YOUR MOM SAYS MONEY DOESN'T GROW ON TREES

BECAUSE SHE WORKS HARD FOR HER MONEY.
ON HER KNEES

DAD CHASES MONEY ALL DAY AT HIS JOB

CREATING WEALTH FOR HIS CEO ROB

SOME SAY THE BEST THINGS IN LIFE ARE FREE

"IN THE LONG RUN, A WIFE COSTS MORE MONEY THAN A HOE."

ASK ANY PIMP OR DIVORCE LAWYER, AND THEY'LL DISAGREE

GRANNY SAYS A PENNY SAVED IS A PENNY EARNED

BUT CLIPPING COUPONS DOESN'T FIX HER MONEY CONCERNS

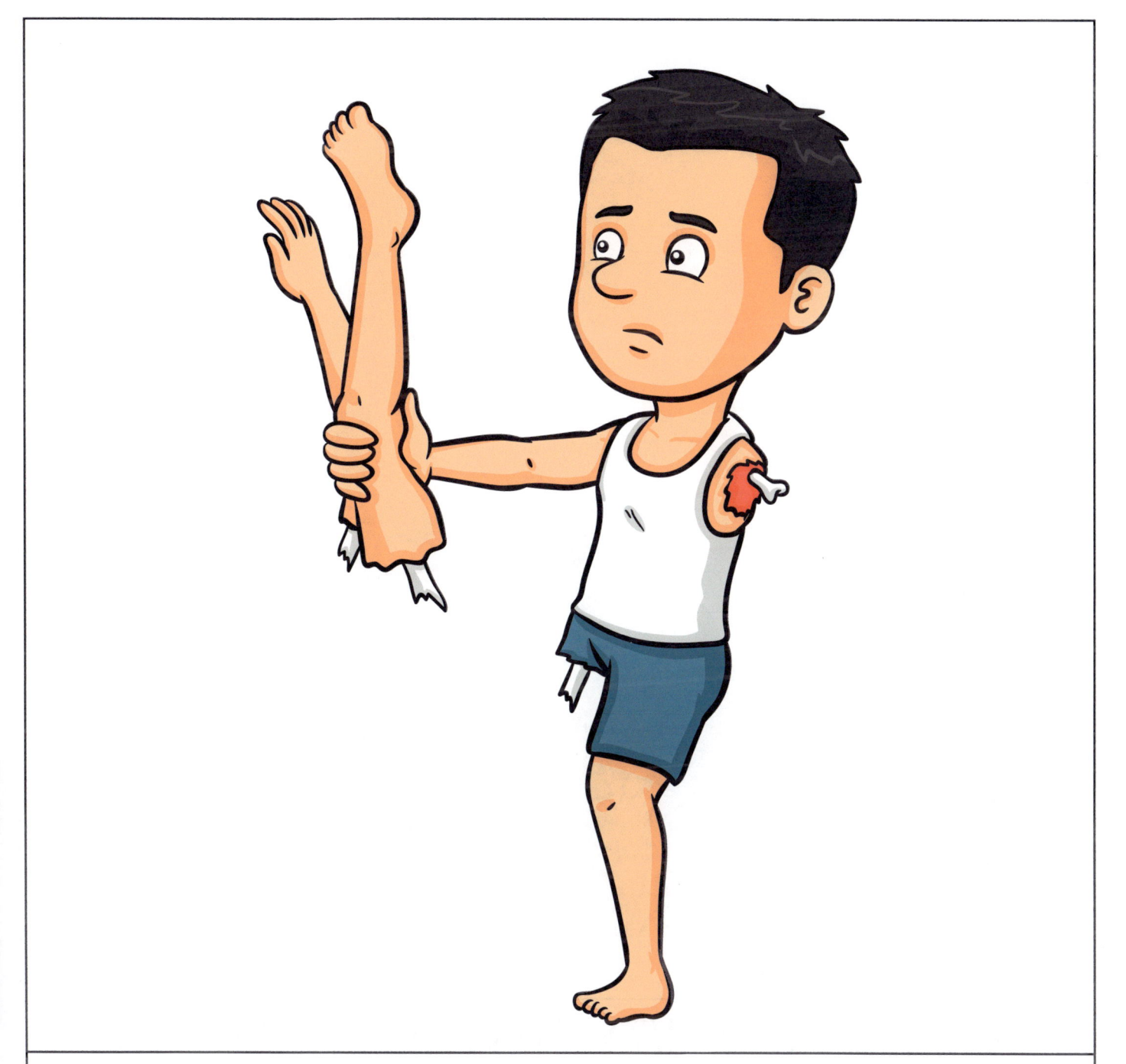

PEOPLE SAY THINGS COST AN ARM AND A LEG

WITH A SCARCITY MINDSET. THEY'LL ALWAYS HAVE TO BEG

LIFE IS EASY WHEN YOU SEE MONEY IS ABUNDANT

SO DON'T GET STUCK IN A JOB THAT'S REDUNDANT

KIDS ARE TOLD TO NOT BE GREEDY

BUT SHARING TOO MUCH WILL JUST LEAVE YOU NEEDY

"MONEY IS THE ROOT OF ALL EVIL."
THAT'S WHAT PEOPLE SAY.

THAT MINDSET WILL ALWAYS CHASE MONEY AWAY

DON'T LISTEN TO ADVICE FROM PEOPLE WITH NO BUCKS

MONEY COMES EASILY WHEN YOU MAKE YOUR OWN LUCK!

MOMS ONLY FANS

NEW BEGINNINGS FROM DIFFICULT CHOICES

Brad Gosse

MOM AND DAD WERE FIGHTING TOO MUCH

SO DAD PACKED HIS BAGS. HE SAID SHE WAS SUCH...

A BITCH ALL THE TIME. ARE THE WORDS THAT HE SPOKE

NOW THEY'RE DIVORCED. AND HE LEFT YOUR MOM BROKE

DIFFICULT CHOICES YOUR MOMMY MUST MAKE

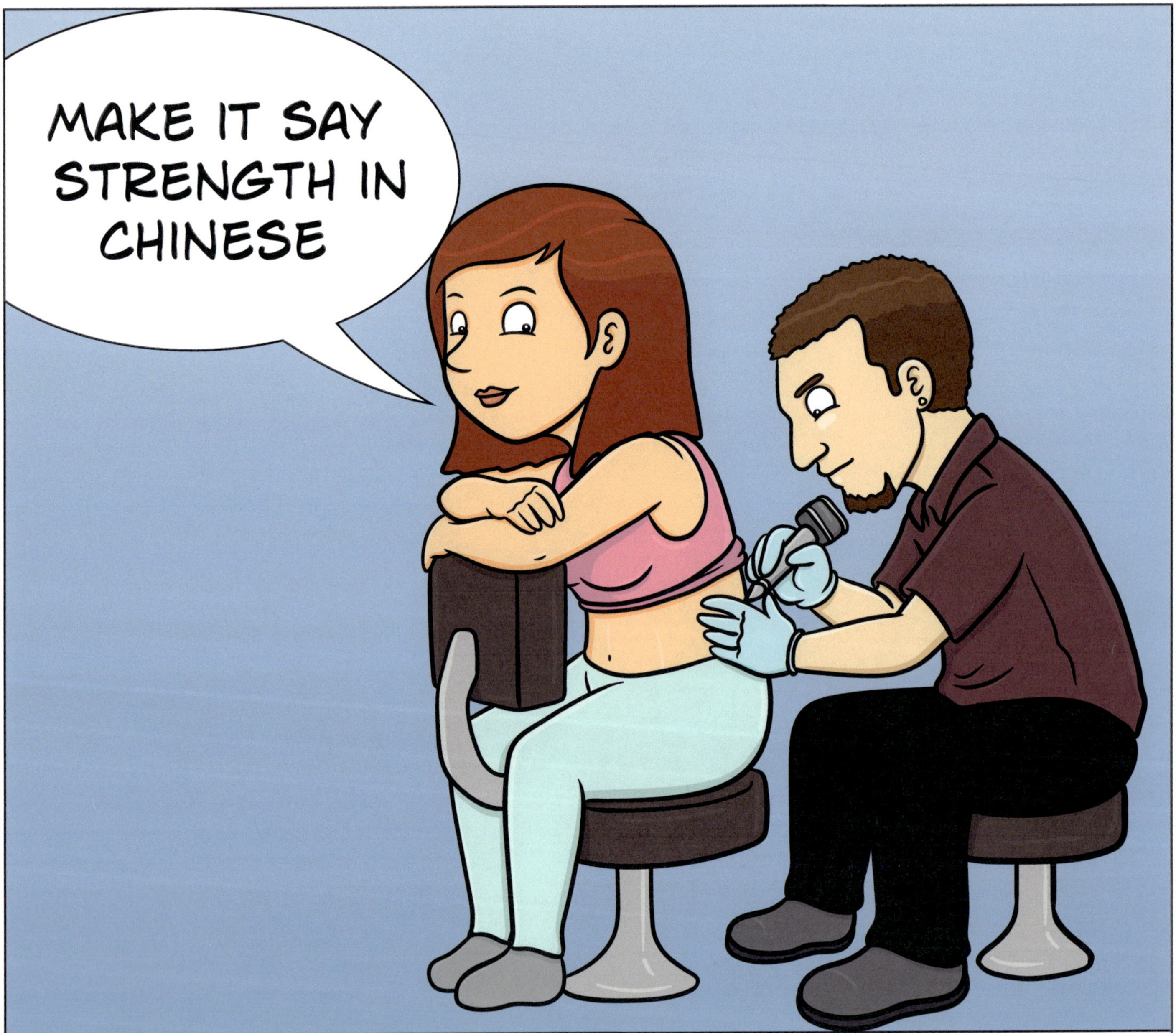

BUT SHE'S A STRONG LADY- SO MAKE NO MISTAKE

SHE WENT OUT SHOPPING FOR SEXY COSTUMES

THEN PUT A BACKDROP AND LIGHTS IN HER ROOM

AND THEN SHE PICKED UP A FANCY NEW CAM

YEP. YOU GUESSED IT. MOM'S ON ONLY FANS

SHE'S MAKING VIDEOS IN VARIOUS CLOTHES

WHAT SHE DOES ON MEETUPS.
NOBODY KNOWS

BUT YOUR MOMMY NO LONGER STRUGGLES WITH RENT

HER ACCOUNT HAS MADE IT TO THE TOP 5 PERCENT

MURDER HORNETS
FROM ASIAN INVASION TO OVER RATED SENSATION

Brad Gosse

MURDER HORNETS STARTED WITH A BIG SCARE

ONE STING PROMISED GREAT DESPAIR

ONCE YOU WERE ALL THE RAGE

UNTIL COVID-19 TOOK THE STAGE

2020 SHOULD HAVE BEEN YOUR GLOW UP YEAR

TERRORIZING PEOPLE WITH YOUR UNIQUE BRAND OF FEAR

STORIES OF YOUR SPREES OF MURDER

REPLACED BY EXHAUSTED HEALTH CARE WORKERS

EVERYONE STAYED HOME THIS YEAR

PREVENTING YOU FROM SPREADING FEAR

OUT SHINED BY ANOTHER ASIAN INVASION

COVID-19 WAS THE BIG OCCASION

IN THE BEGINNING, FEAR WAS EVOKED

NOW YOU HAVE BECOME A JOKE

OK BOOMER

IT'S NOT AN AGE. IT'S AN ATTITUDE

BRAD GOSSE

BOOMER ALWAYS COMPLAINS AT THE STORE

WHEN YESTERDAY'S SPECIAL ISN'T AVAILABLE ANYMORE

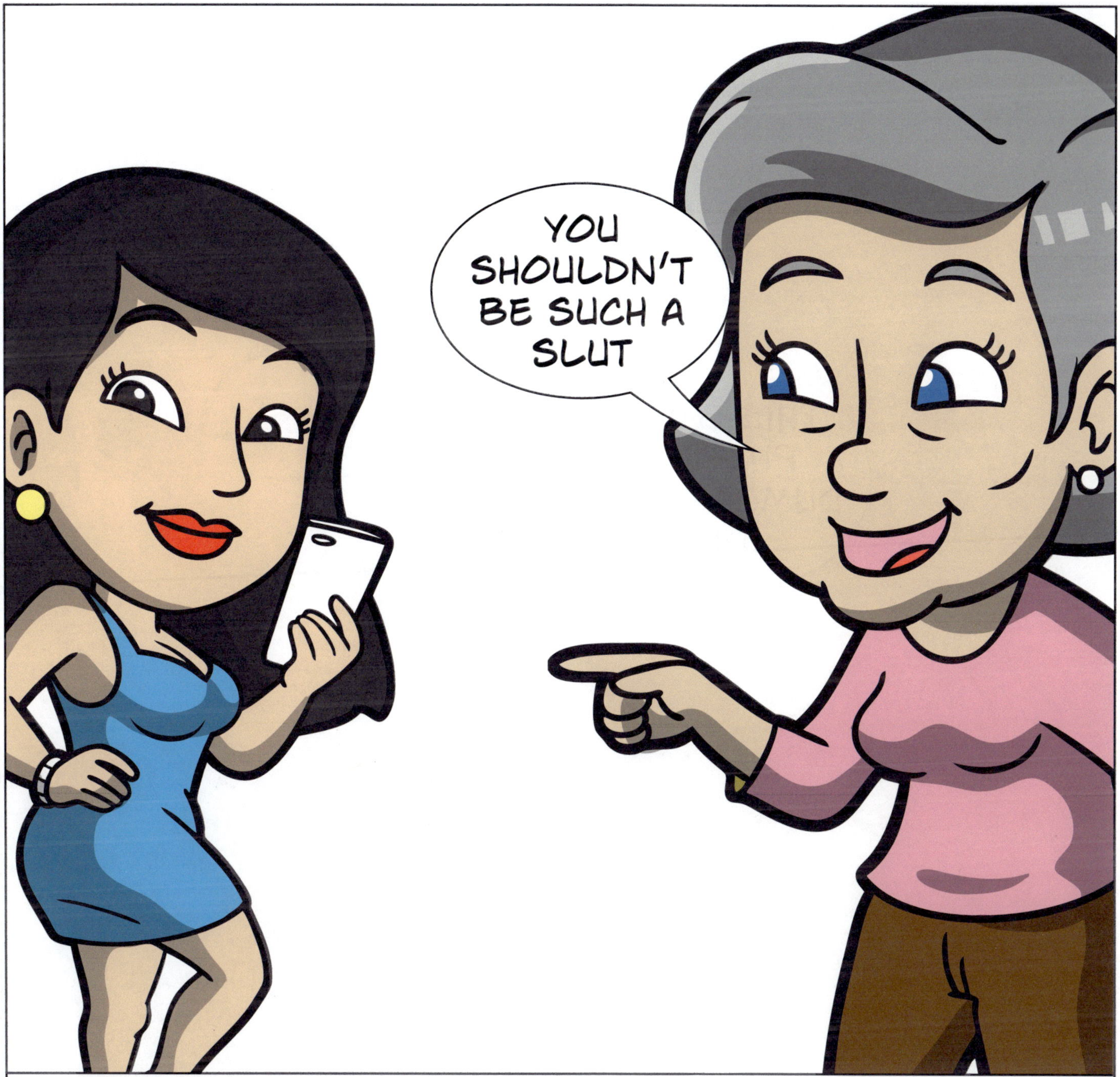

BOOMER GIVES UNSOLICITED ADVICE

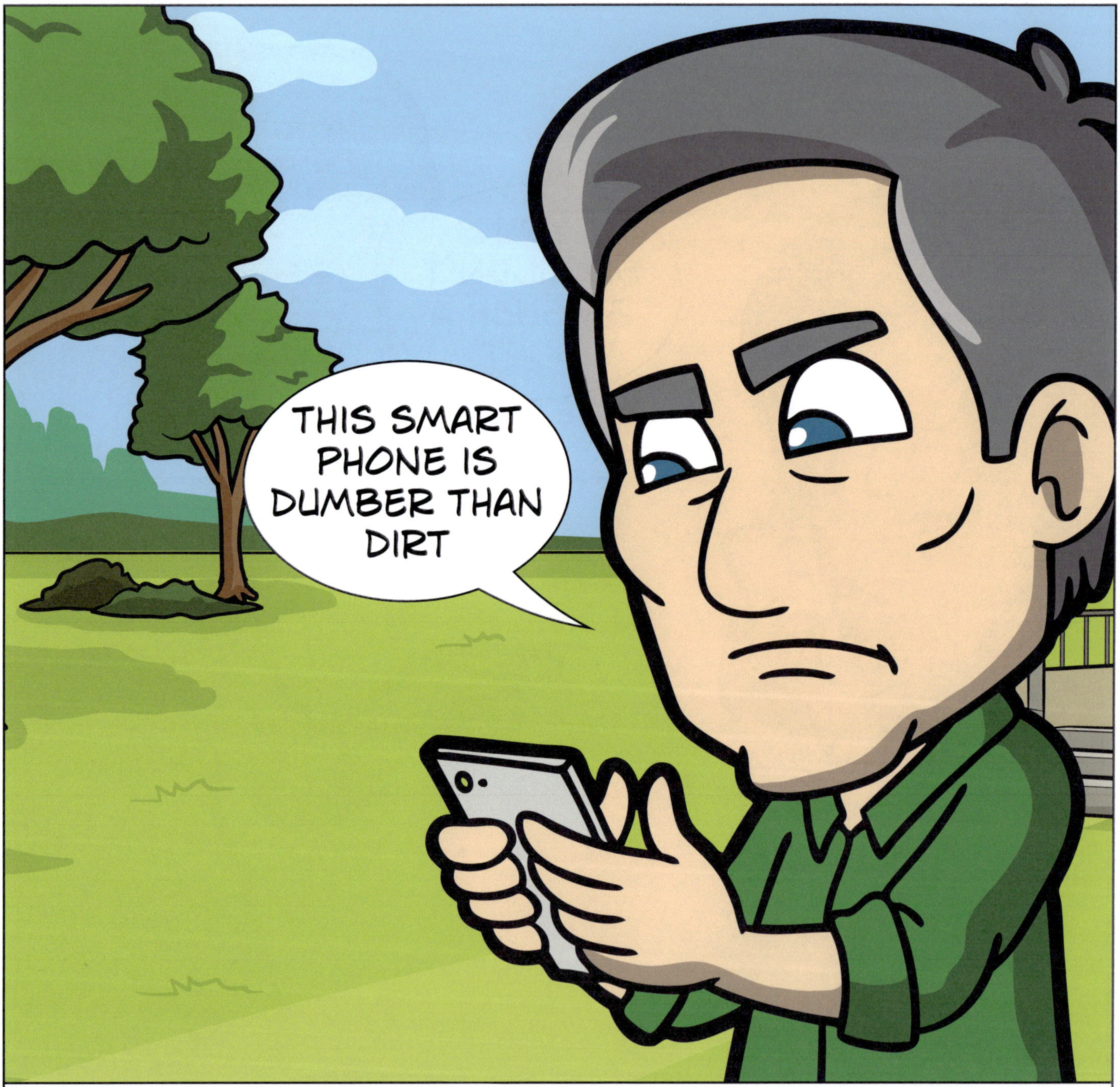

BOOMER ALWAYS STRUGGLES WITH HIS DEVICE

BOOMER DEMANDS YOUR SUPERVISOR

AND NEVER ORDERS THE APPETIZER

BOOMER TRAVELS ALL THE TIME

AND STILL MAINTAINS A LANDLINE

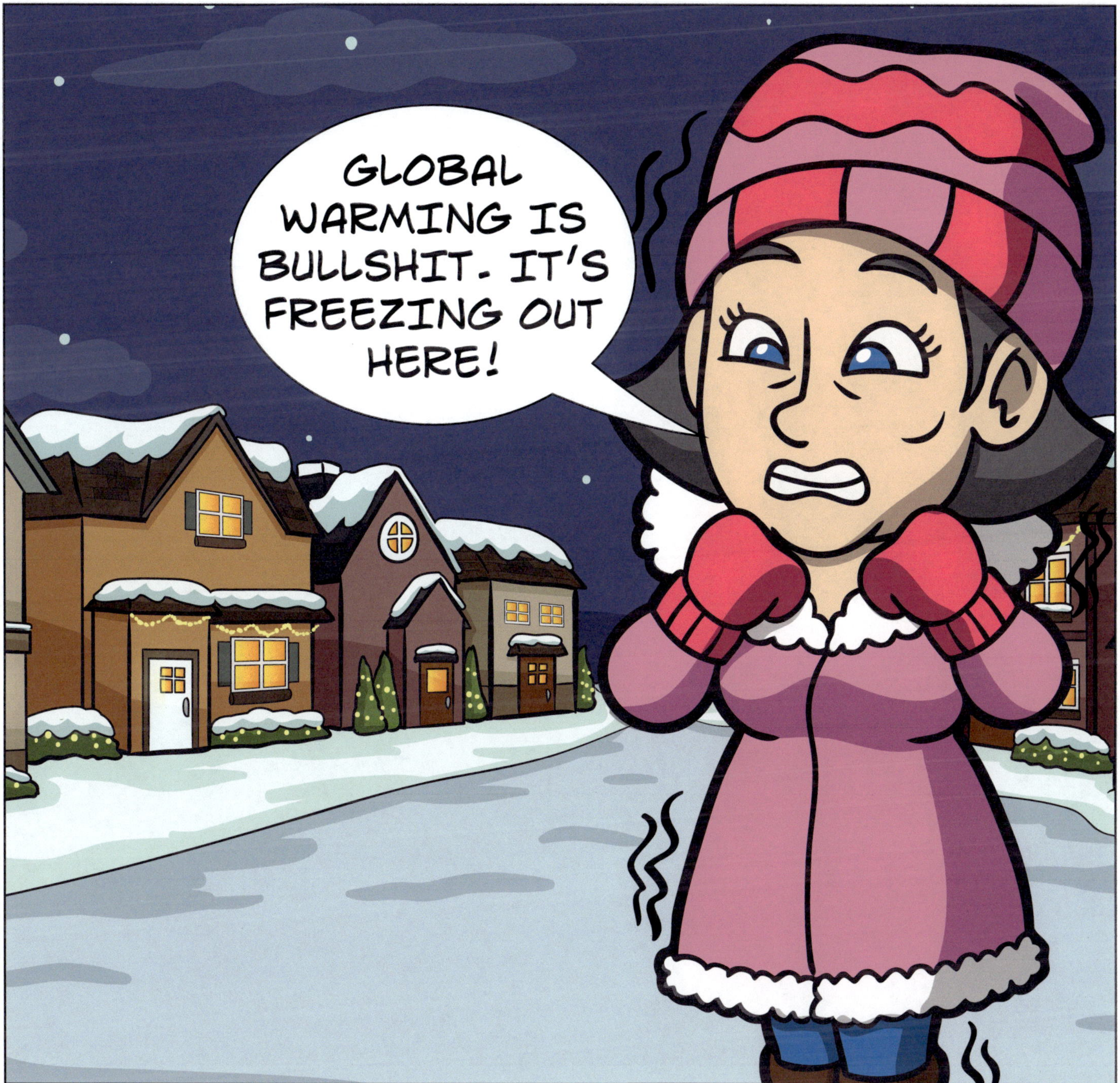

BOOMER DENIES CLIMATE CHANGE

AND ALWAYS GOES TO THE DRIVING RANGE

BOOMER MAINTAINS A PERFECT LAWN

TO HELP FORGET THE CHILDREN HAVE GONE

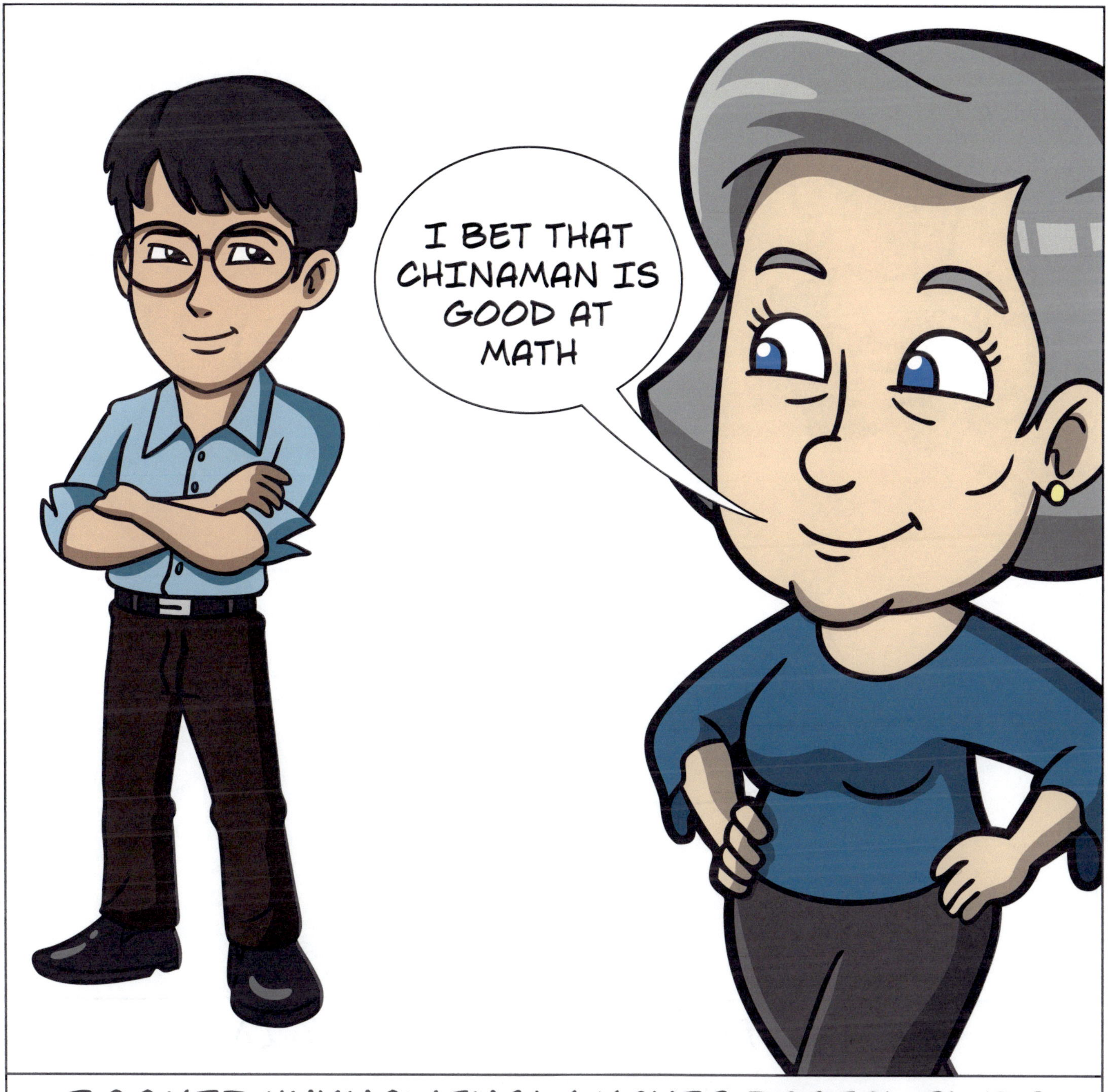

BOOMER UNKNOWINGLY MAKES RACIAL SLURS

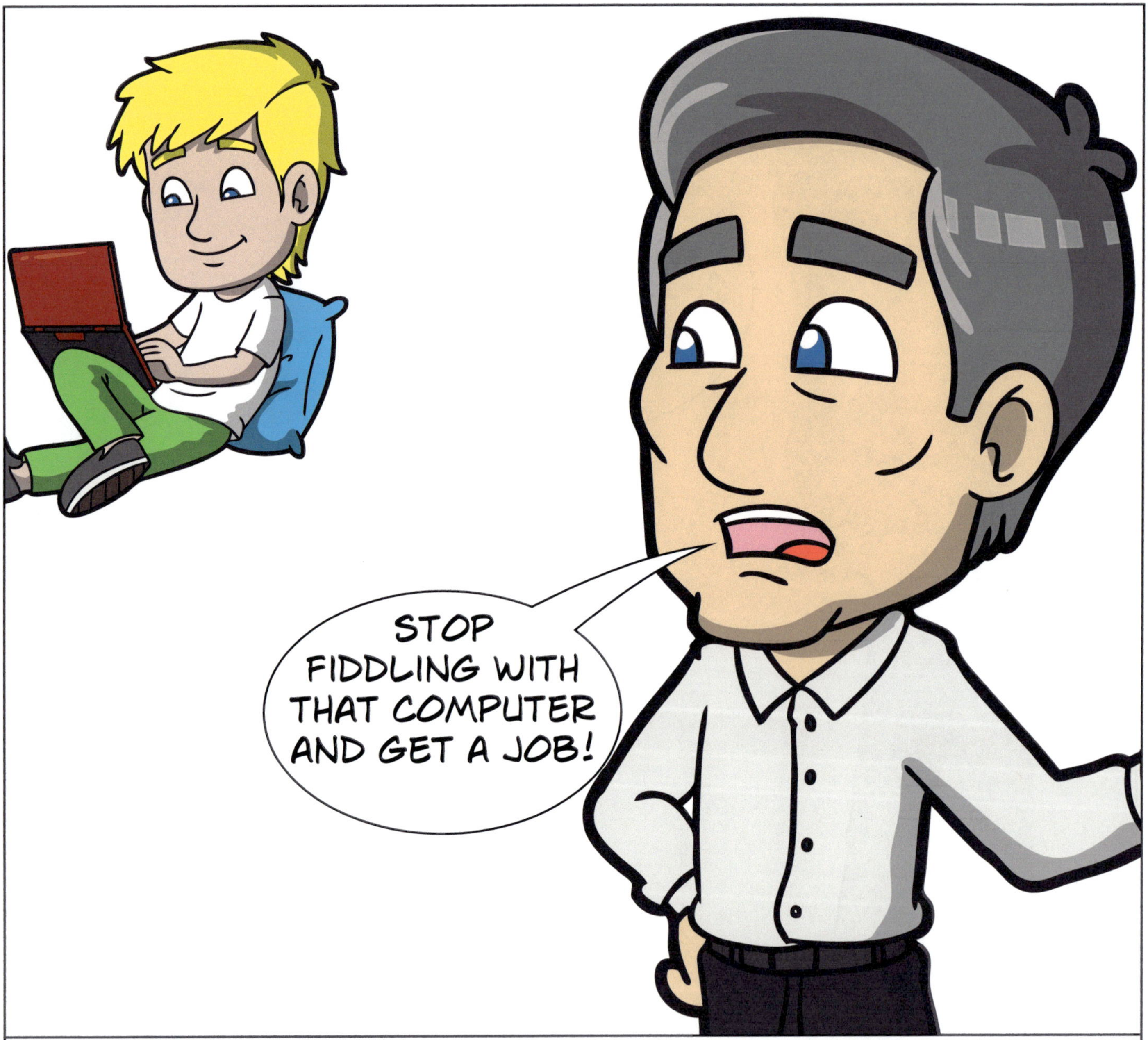

AND DOESN'T BELIEVE IN ENTREPRENEURS

"I'M ON A FIXED INCOME"

BOOMER WANTS TO TELL YOU SHE'S BROKE

THAT GUYS FACE IS SLIPPING
AND RECOGNIZES THE SIGNS OF A STROKE

BOOMER STILL READS THE MORNING PAPER

AND PROTESTS AGAINST NEW SKYSCRAPERS

BOOMER ALWAYS TRIMS HIS HEDGES

"WANNA TRY SOME BBQ?"

"DO YOU HAVE A PERMIT TO COOK HERE?"

AGAINST BLACK PEOPLE, SHE ALWAYS ALLEGES

OUR'S BABY

THE ONLY CHILD YOUR STEPMOM LOVES

Brad Gosse

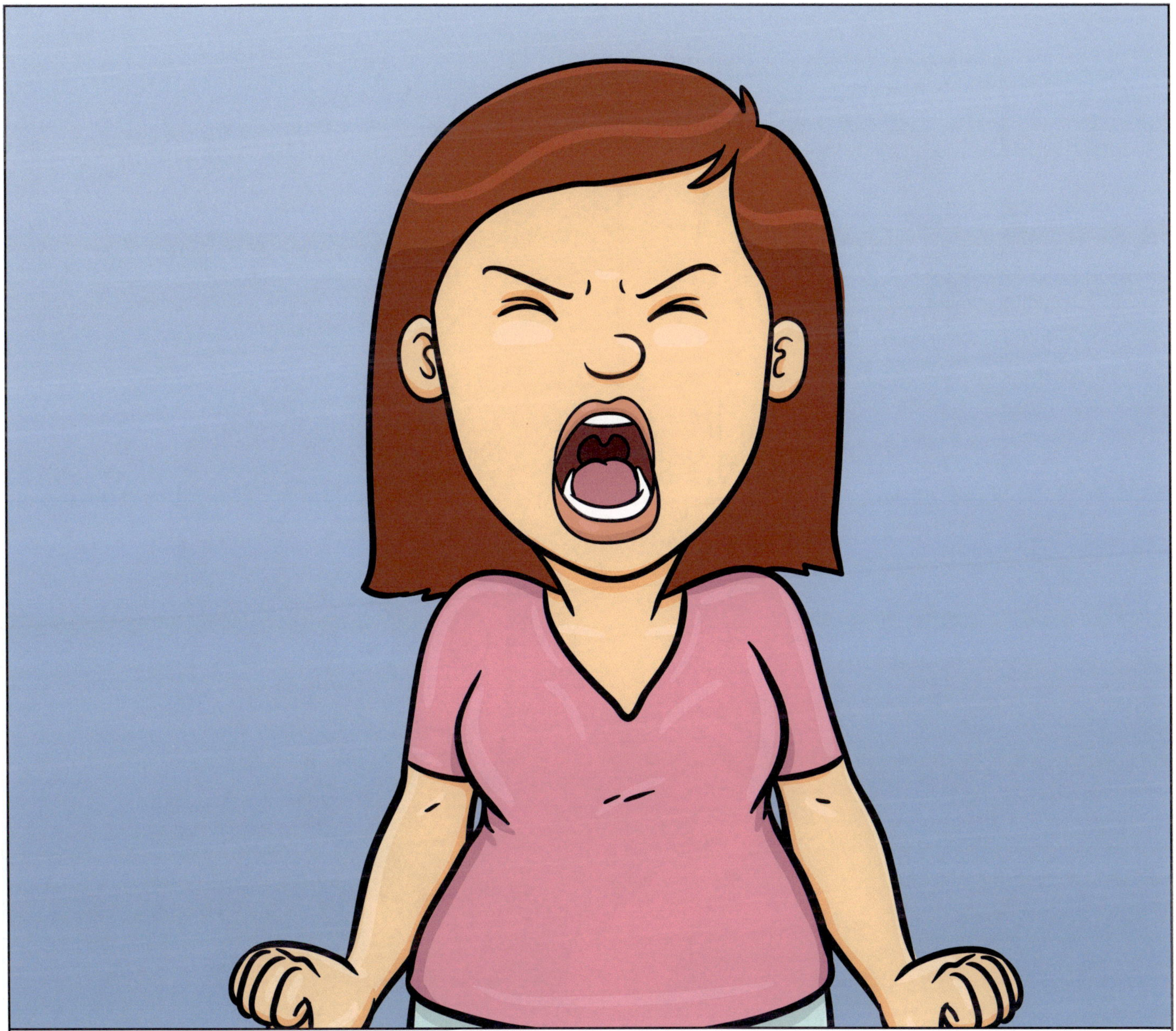

YOUR NEW STEP MOM SEEMS NICE

SHE MAKES YOUR DAD HAPPY

BUT SHE WANTS MORE FROM HIM

IT'LL MAKE YOUR LIFE CRAPPY

SHE PRAYED EVERY DAY

FOR SOMEONE PLEASE MAYBE

TO DELIVER A MAN

WHO COULD GIVE HER A BABY

YOUR DAD HAS OLD SPERM

BUT YOUR STEPMOM CAN STILL

CARRY A BABY TO TERM

MEET YOUR NEW BROTHER BILL

"OURS BABY" IS WHAT YOUR STEPMOM PROCLAIMS

IN JUST A FEW DAYS

SHE WON'T WANT TO HEAR YOUR NAMES

SHE HAS A BABY WITH HER DNA

SO GO GET A JOB. RIGHT NOW

TODAY!

STEPMOM SAYS IT'S TIME TO MOVE OUT

NOW YOU KNOW WHAT "OURS BABY" IS ACTUALLY ABOUT

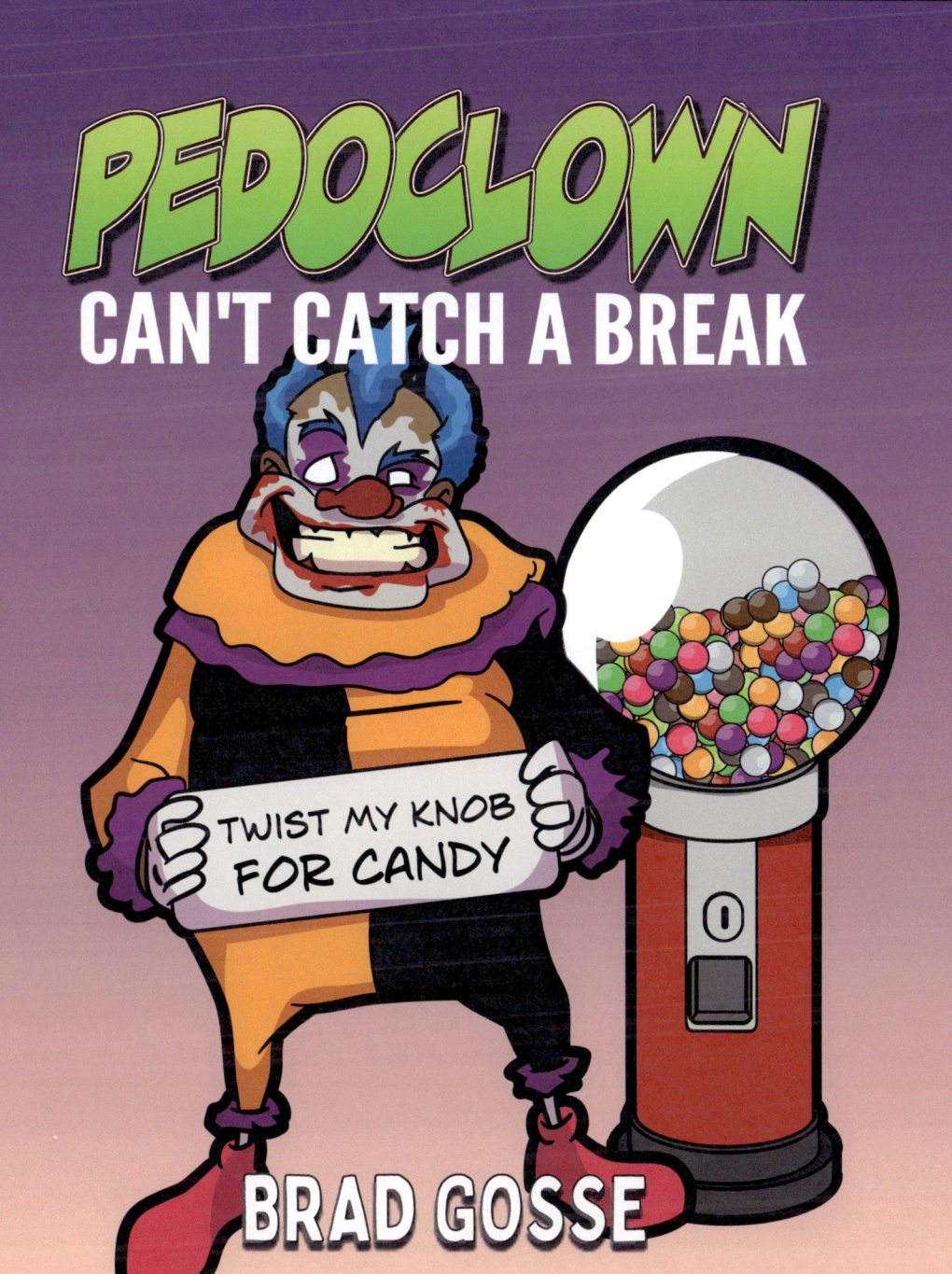

PEDOCLOWN
CAN'T CATCH A BREAK

BRAD GOSSE

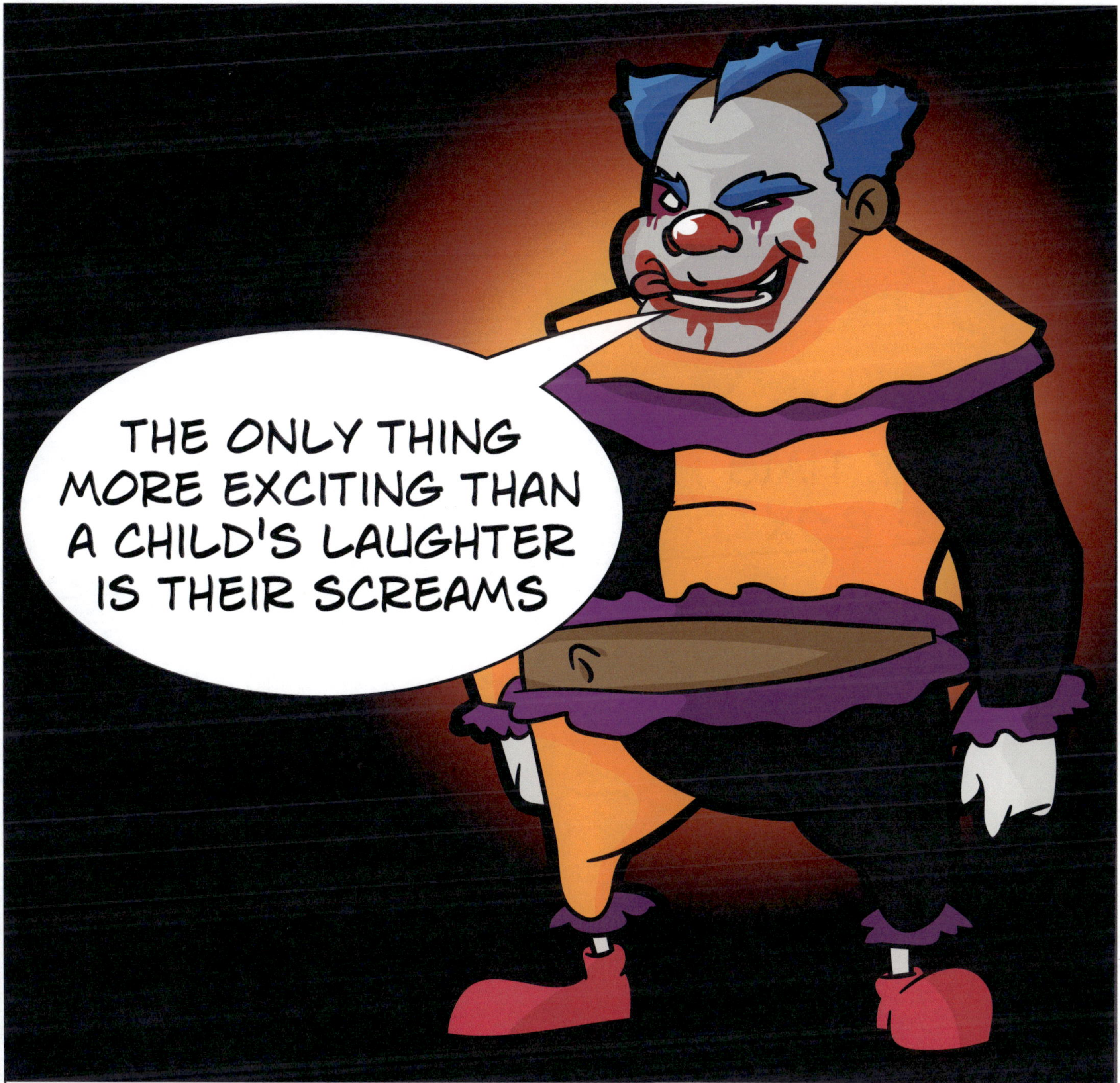

PEDOCLOWN SAYS INAPPROPRIATE THINGS

"TRY MY SLEEPY TIME JUICE BOX"

HE CARRIES NEEDLES THAT REALLY STING

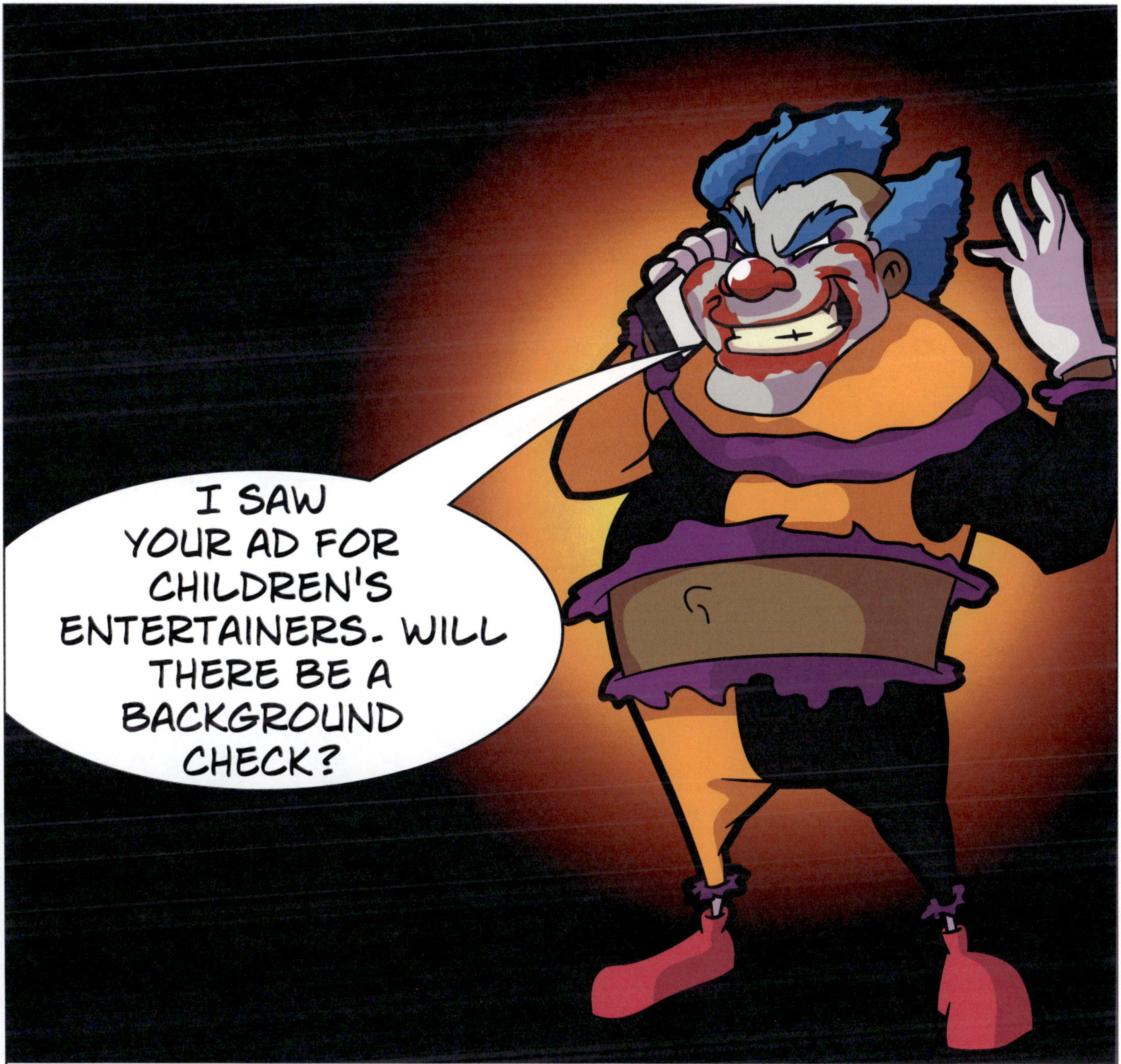

PEDOCLOWN HAS A SKETCHY PAST

KIDS LOVE ME... EXCPET THE ONES THAT TELL.
AND SCARES POTENTIAL CUSTOMERS AWAY FAST

"IT LOOKS EVEN BIGGER IN LITTLE HANDS"

HE MAKES BALLOONS IN THE SHAPE OF A PENIS

AND CONSIDERS HIMSELF A MARKETING GENIUS

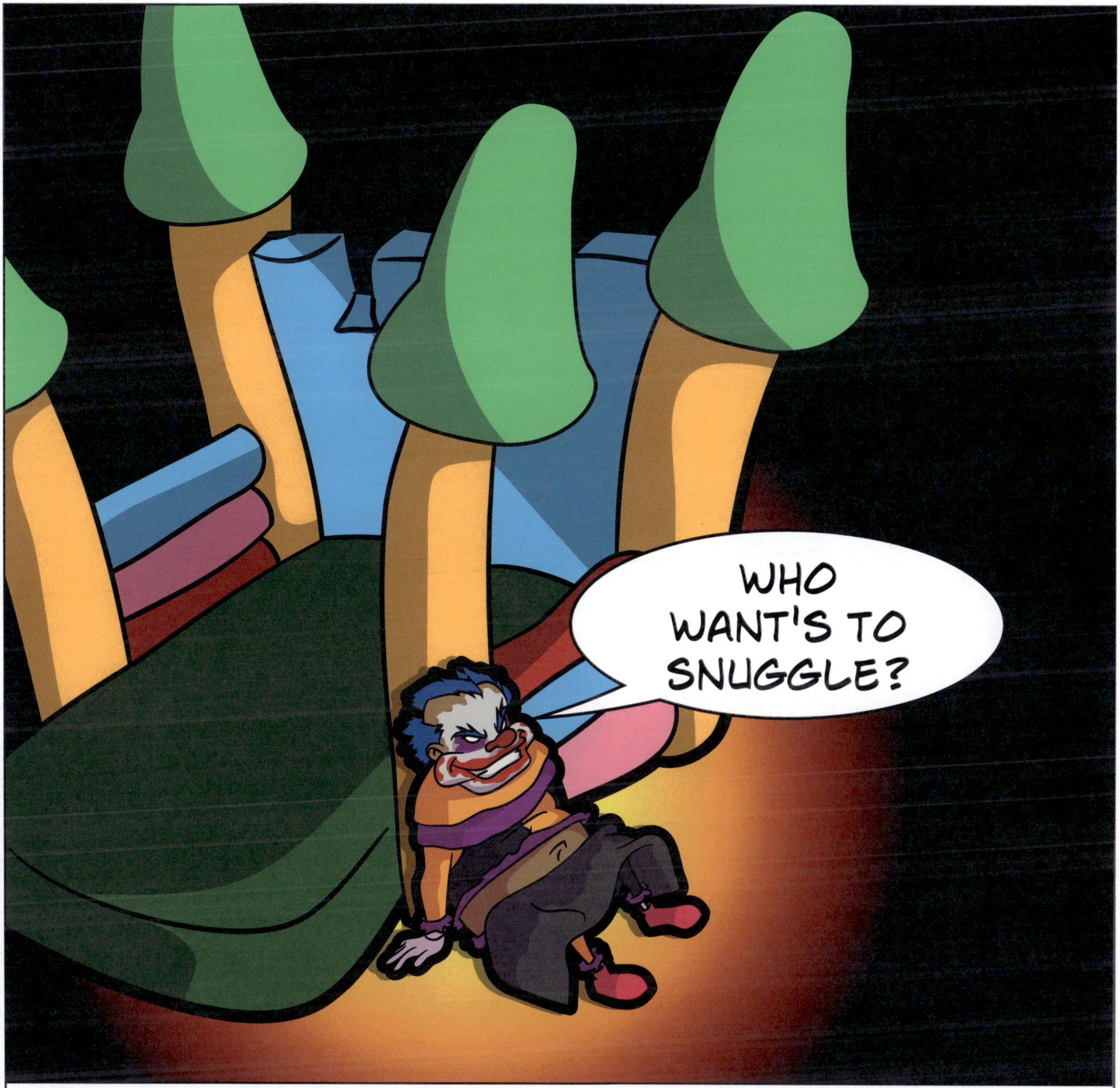

PEDOCLOWN INVESTED IN A BOUNCY CASTLE

BIG DAY
WAITING OUTSIDE THE
PUBLIC SCHOOL FOR
RECESS
BUT FINDING NEW CUSTOMERS IS ALWAYS A HASSLE

HE SILENCES CHILDREN WITH CHLOROFORM

AND ALWAYS OFFERS YOU FRESH POPCORN

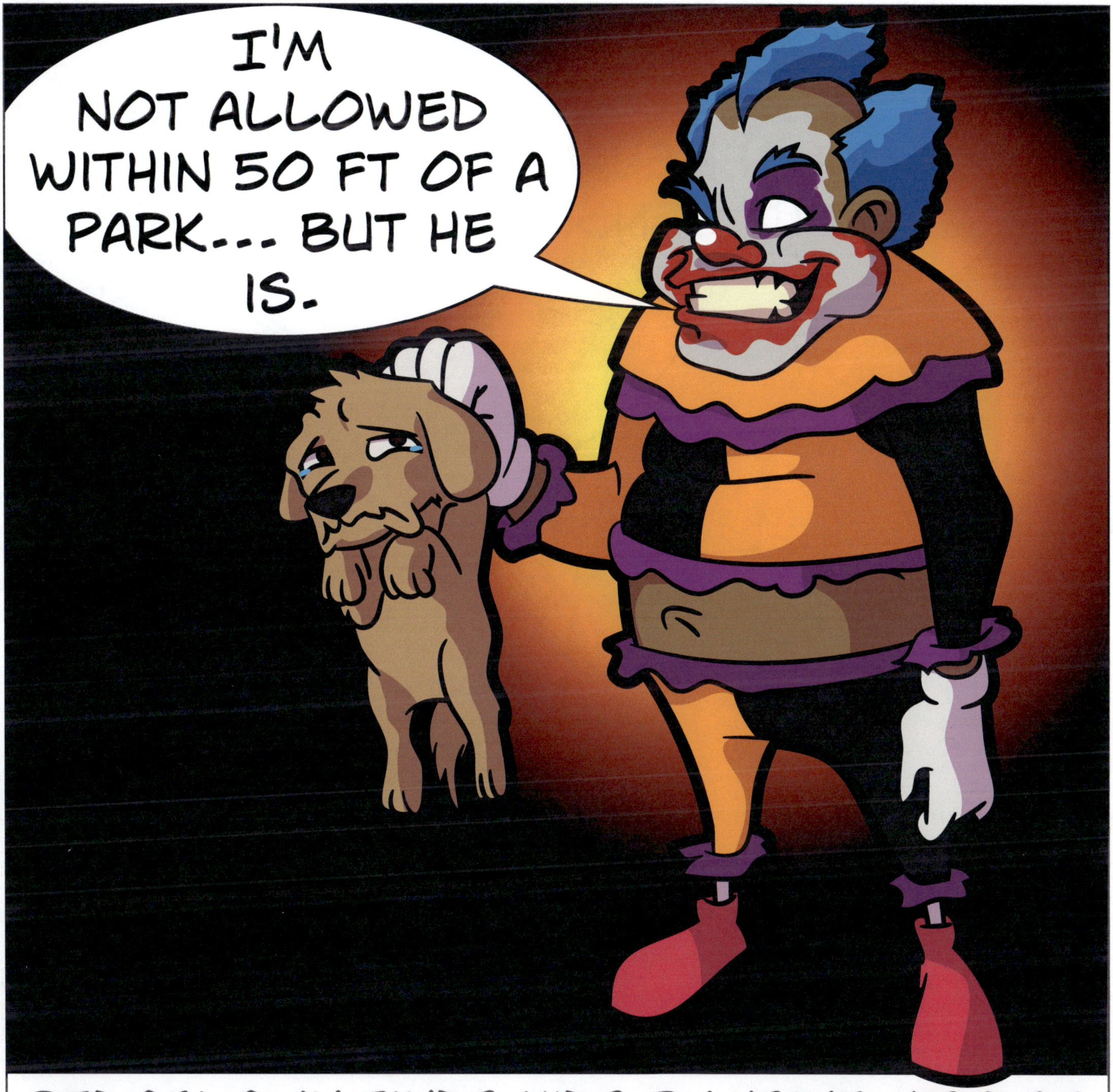

PEDOCLOWN FINDS KIDS BY USING HIS DOG

YOU CAN'T SPELL CONSENSUAL WITHOUT SENSUAL
AND HAS BIZARRE INTERNAL DIALOGUE

> THE SWEETEST TREATS ARE NICE AND DEEP

HE ALWAYS OFFERS A VARIETY OF TREATS

"FREE INTERACTIVE PUPPET SHOWS"

AND HIS PUPPET SHOWS SIMPLY CAN'T BE BEAT

PEDOCLOWN IS ALWAYS DRINKING LIKE A FISH

BECAUSE HE'S ON A PERMANENT SEX OFFENDER LIST

"ALL ABOARD THE SECRET, NO PANTS, FUN TIME EXPRESS; NEXT STOP MY APARTMENT"

HE TRIES TO CONVINCE YOU WITH A VAN FULL OF CAKE

BUT PEDOCLOWN JUST CAN'T CATCH A BREAK

SELF ISOLATION
16 WAYS TO PREVENT BOREDOM

Brad Gosse

USE THE INTERNET TO MAKE FRIENDS WITH NEW STRANGERS

THROW SHARP OBJECTS AT YOUR BROTHER. IGNORING THE DANGER

AIM A LASER POINTER FROM YOUR BEDROOM WINDOW AT PLANES

TRY JUMPING OFF YOUR ROOF AGAIN AND AGAIN

PRACTICE THROWING A BOWLING BALL AT YOUR BABY BROTHER

TRY FIRING SHARP ARROWS AT YOUR MOTHER

TRY SOME NEW DANCE MOVES OUT IN YOUR BATHROOM

MAKE A SMALL CAMPFIRE IN YOUR MESSY BEDROOM

TRY PUTTING A FINGER INTO YOUR CAT'S BUTT

TRY CALLING YOUR MOTHER A DIRTY OLD SLUT

IF HE DRIVES YOU CRAZY. TELL YOUR DAD TO GO TO HELL

PUSH YOUR MOM DOWN THE STAIRS. TELL THE COPS THAT SHE FELL

HIDE YOUR BABY SISTER FROM YOUR PARENTS IN THE ATTIC

IF YOU DON'T GET YOUR WAY TRY BEING DRAMATIC

A GREAT CURE FOR BOREDOM IS TO EAT SOME JUNK FOOD

TRY STICKING YOUR DAD'S BUTT TO THE TOILET WITH GLUE

STD'S & YOU
LEARNING FROM THE ANIMALS AT THE ZOO

Brad Gosse

DAD HAD UNPROTECTED BUTT SEX WITH A STRANGE MAN

HIS VISIT TO THE DOCTOR WASN'T PLANNED

SO HE TOOK YOU TO THE ZOO SO HE COULD EXPLAIN

GARY THE GONORRHEA GORILLA

GONORRHEA CAUSES YELLOW DISCHARGE AND PAIN

REMEMBER WHEN MOM BROUGHT HOME THAT STRANGER?

| ALBERT THE AIDS ALPACA |

SHE GOT THE AIDS. NOT KNOWING THE DANGER

THAT UNPROTECTED SEX CAN BRING TO YOU

SO WRAP UP YOUR JUNK WHATEVER YOU DO

SEYMOUR THE CHLAMYDIA CATFISH

CHLAMYDIA MAY STOP YOU FROM HAVING KIDS

PUBIC LICE PIGEON

CRABS AKA PUBLIC LICE IS EASY FOR YOU TO RID

SANDY THE SYPHILIS SQUIRREL

SYPHILIS STARTS OUT AS A FEW PAINLESS SORES

| HEATHER THE HPV HIPPO |

HPV CAN END UP BEING SO MUCH MORE

GENITAL WARTS GIRAFFEY

ALSO CALLED GENITAL WARTS IT MAY LEAD TO CANCER

HAMMERS THE HERPES HAMSTER

HERPES HAS NO CURE. NOW YOU HAVE THE ANSWERS

ABOUT STDS SO NOW YOU KNOW

TO ALWAYS WEAR CONDOMS WHEN YOU SLEEP WITH THE HOES

WHY MOMMY HITS DADDY

KIDS GUIDE TO UNDERSTANDING ALCOHOLISM

Brad Gosse

WHEN MOM COMES HOME SHE DOESN'T EXPECT MUCH

A CLEAN BATHROOM

AND YOUR FATHERS GENTLE TOUCH

EVEN THOUGH YOUR DADDY WORKS HARD

SHE EXPECTED HIM TO CLEAN THE POOPS IN THE YARD

AFTER MOM STARTS DRINKING WINE

WITH YOUR FATHER SHE DRAWS THE LINE

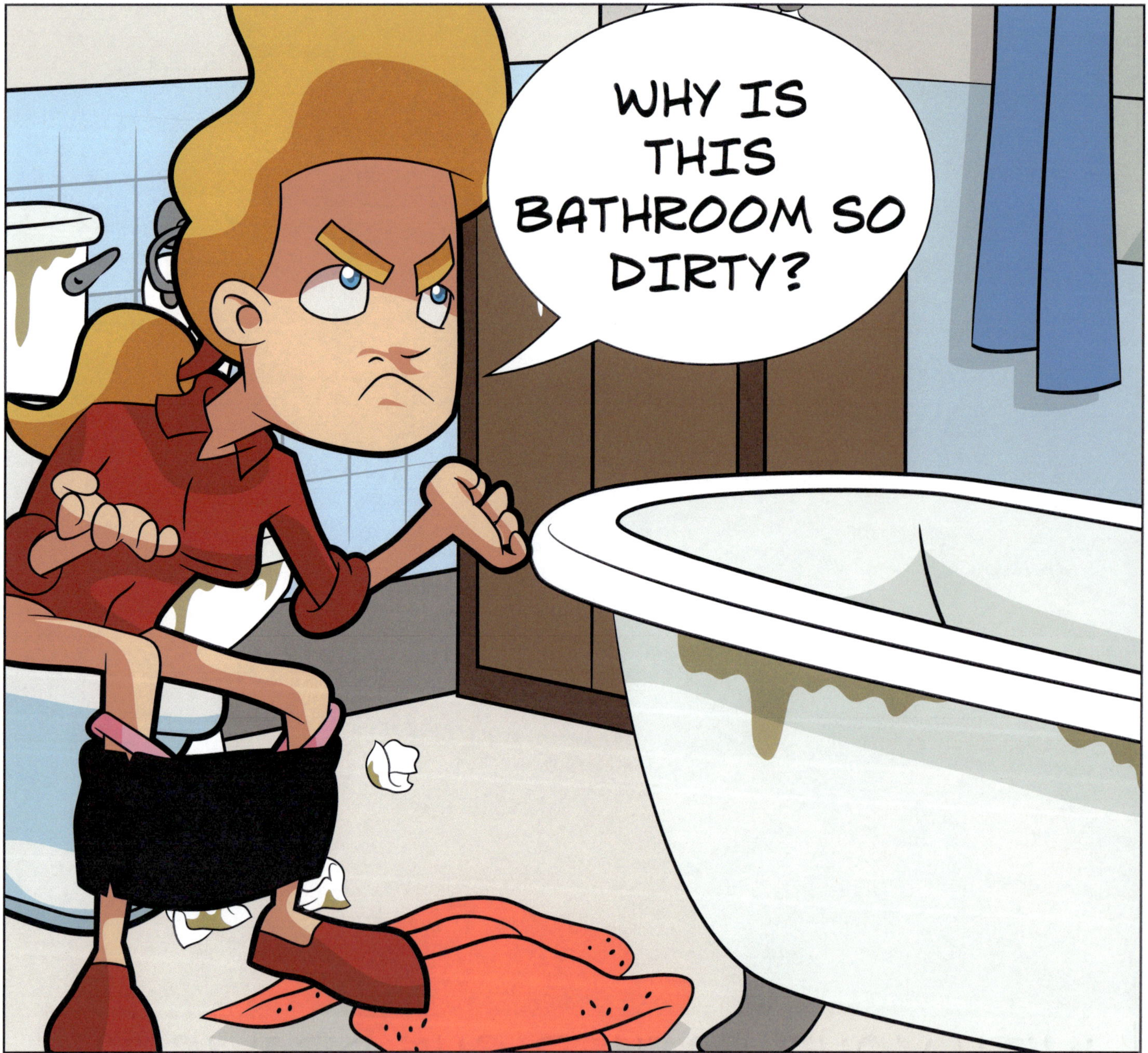

ONCE MOM TAKES A BREAK TO PEE

YOU AND YOUR DAD HAD BETTER FLEE

TO THE LAWYER YOU MUST GO

BEFORE MOM'S ANGER PLATEAUS

AND SHE BEATS YOUR DADDY WITH HER FISTS

BECAUSE SHE CAN'T CONTROL HER DRUNKEN FITS

DRINKING IS YOUR MOM'S ISSUE

NOW GO AND GET YOUR DAD A TISSUE

If you want to reach me.

TW: @bradgosse
IG: @bradgosse
FB: @bradgosse
TIKTOK: @bradgosse
Youtube: @BradGosse

If you want clipart from this book.
@vectortoons
VectorToons.com

Brad Gosse

THE END. WRITTEN BY BRAD GOSSE

Made in United States
Troutdale, OR
03/15/2025